FORGIVE ME

To: Joyce—

Raise the Belief!

♥, Mary-Kaitlyn
Brown

Mark 11:25

FORGIVE ME

MARY-KAITLYN BROWN

TATE PUBLISHING & Enterprises

Published by Tate Publishing & Enterprises, LLC
127 E. Trade Center Terrace | Mustang, Oklahoma 73064 USA
1.888.361.9473 | www.tatepublishing.com

Tate Publishing is committed to excellence in the publishing industry. The company reflects the philosophy established by the founders, based on Psalm 68:11,
"The Lord gave the word and great was the company of those who published it."

Book design copyright © 2011 by Tate Publishing, LLC. All rights reserved.
Cover design by Kenna Davis
Interior design by Stephanie

Published in the United States of America

ISBN: 978-1-61777-465-2
1. Fiction / Christian / General   2. Fiction / Christian / Suspense
11.03.21

DEDICATION

To everyone who believed in me,
　　To everyone who offered their love and support,
　　　　And to the one who never stopped forgiving…
　　　　　God, this one's for you.

ACKNOWLEDGMENTS

To my family, who has supported me all my life. You have played a huge part in the success of this book, and in who I have become as a person.

To Nanny and Geena, Mimi and Papa, your endless love and support are the things that have gotten me where I am today.

To Mom, Dad, and Troy, because we all know I could've never finished this book if it weren't for you. Thank you for giving me that extra push and for always showing me support for the things I love to do. Thank you for believing in me.

To my closest friends, thank you all so much. You have been with me through everything, and have inspired me greatly. I will never forget the love and support you all gave so freely. You are my true sisters.

And last but not least, this is to you God. You are the one and only reason I have made it this far. I am so blessed to be able to spread your Word to others. Thank you for your merciful love, and your unending forgiveness. I know that you will never leave nor forsake me, and I find comfort in knowing that you will always be there for me. Thank you for making all my dreams come true.

This book is for the people of this world who are struggling with loss. It's for those who are wrestling with forgiveness. I can't say it's easy to forgive; in fact, it's probably the hardest thing we all might ever have to do. But instead of listening to me, why not hear what God has to say about it? He spoke through me as I wrote this book.

I hope you all will read this and open your hearts to a world with no more pain. To a place where love is never-ending and peace is just a prayer away. All we have to do is forgive.

Love forever and many blessings,
Mary-Kaitlyn Brown

CARLEY

"I'm leavin'!" My mom called from the doorway of our nineteenth century Victorian mansion. I sat in our formal dining room eating a bowl of cereal, alone. "Okay," I said. "See you tonight." The only reply I received was the slamming of our front door as my mom made her way down our driveway to her shiny BMW parked out front. I dropped my spoon into the nearly untouched bowl of cereal and walked to the kitchen sink. I began scraping off the remnants of my breakfast and turned on the garbage disposal, shoving down the bits of food that clung to the porcelain sides. I turned off the disposal and walked upstairs to finish getting ready for school. When I reached my bedroom, I headed straight for my closet. Opening the tall French doors, I began surveying my potential outfits for the day. I quickly spotted the perfect attire: a white spaghetti strap top with a sheer pink cover-up, a pair of designer jeans, and my favorite white heels. After getting dressed and then fixing my hair and makeup, I finally made my way back downstairs just in time to hear my boyfriend's car horn honk out front. I peeked out the window before grabbing my backpack. Slinging the black bag over my shoulders, I quickly made my way out of the front door, leaving behind a lonely morning.

"Hey, C." Jason smiled as I threw my bag in the back seat of his jet black Camaro. Climbing into the seat next to him, I gently pecked him on the cheek and offered a warm smile. "Hey," I replied. Jason laughed heartily at my meek sense of affection. We were quiet as we made our journey to the school about fifteen minutes away. Jason was the first to strike up conversation. "So you're coming tonight, right?"

I had been dreading this question for the entire week, and I was not ready for it, even when the time finally presented itself.

"Uhm…" I stuttered.

"Come on, C. Please. I really want to go to this party, and I can't go by myself," Jason pleaded.

"Jay, you know I can't come tonight. Mom finally promised to have dinner with me. Just the two of us. You know how long I've waited for this. If I pass up this chance, who knows when she'll be willing to hang out again?"

Jason huffed and looked out the window. "Yeah I know," he whispered.

"Aw, Jay, don't be like this. Please? You know this isn't my fault," I said.

"Yeah it's fine, really. I'll just go with Will and some of the guys. It's cool."

"All right, well, you know I would come if I could, right?" I asked.

"Yeah, sure," Jason responded.

I could detect a hint of sarcasm in his voice but I didn't bring it up. I wasn't prepared for an argument this early. Instead, I opened the car door and stepped out into the throng of students swarming North Kale High School. "Bye Jay." I smiled.

He waved single-handedly at me and drove away to find a parking spot.

Annoyed, I made my way through the people in the front of the school, all rushing to get to class before the bell rang. I finally made my way through the swarms of students and into my first period class, biology. I had failed biology sophomore and junior year and was braving the course yet again, my senior year. I walked into a classroom full of freshman and sophomores, and a few scattered juniors. I was by far the dumbest kid in the class.

"Hey, Carley." A few sophomore guys whistled as I walked by. I laughed to myself and headed to my desk in the row by the windows. "Good morning class," my teacher began. This was going to be a long day.

Six hours later and a backpack full of new homework assignments for the weekend had me celebrating the freedom of a Friday after school. I ran to the usual parking space for Jason's car and met him and a few of his friends hovering around. "Hey, guys." I smiled as I made my way over to the group.

A chorus of "hellos" and "what's ups" serenaded me. I was surprised when Jason walked over and put his arm around my shoulders and kissed me. The guys whistled, and I could feel my cheeks growing hot.

"All right, all right." Jason laughed. "I've got to get Carley home. She's got dinner with her mommy tonight." The guys laughed as I playfully punched Jason in the arm and told him to shut up. We finally said our good-byes to the group and got into the car. Jason pulled out from the parking lot and started driving toward my house.

"That was quite a move you pulled back there, mister," I joked.

"What? Can't a guy show off his girlfriend in front of his totally jealous friends?"

I laughed. "Shut up, Jason. You're so stupid."

He smiled. "No really, I just wanted to apologize for the way I acted this morning. It was immature, and I should've understood that you need some time with your mom."

I stared at my boyfriend in bewilderment. "Really?" I asked.

"Yeah, really. You've been upset lately with your relationship with her, and I should've been more understanding. I'm sorry C."

I could feel a small tear begin to well up in my eye as I smiled warmly at the sweetest guy in the world. I reached for his hand resting on the armrest, and squeezed it ever so slightly, but it was enough to let him know how much I really loved him.

I walked into the front door of my house after saying good-bye to Jason. A broad smile was plastered on my face as I sauntered through the door. Things with him hadn't been this good for a while. He was finally beginning to understand how important it was for me to spend time with my mom. He didn't know how lucky he was. His mom was the sweetest lady in the world. She was always baking cookies and buying gifts for me. She was honestly the most genuine person I had ever met.

My mom on the other hand, well, she worked a lot. She never really had time to bake cookies or buy gifts. When my dad left us when I was little, she was determined to become as independent as possible so she was never left alone again. Mom didn't work when she married dad, so when he left us, we had nothing. After he disappeared, mom worked hard and went back to school, got a good job, and with a little help from friends in the right places, she flew straight to the top. Now CEO of a major financing company, she more than just supported us; she drowned us in the finest luxuries available. My mom was good at making sure I had everything I needed. Well, mostly everything.

It wasn't long after I'd gotten dressed in a new outfit and reapplied my makeup for this long-awaited dinner with my mom when I got a text message on my cell phone. I picked up my phone, lying facedown on my bed, and frowned when I saw the number. It was my mom. I opened the text message, expecting the worst, and that's exactly what I got. Typed, in twenty-first century slang, on the miniscule screen of my cutting-edge phone were the words, "Sorry, can't come 2 dinner 2night got called to meet wit sum old friends of mine. hope u undrstnd. next time. promise." I threw my phone down on the bed, only to have it bounce up and fall onto the floor. How could I be so stupid! How could I let this happen again! Of course she couldn't make it tonight. She was planning on skipping out all along.

Oh well, I thought to myself as I picked up my cell phone from the shag carpeted floor. I punched in Jason's number as anger pulsed through my veins.

His voice was comforting and surprisingly soothing. "Hey, C. What's up?"

I gritted my teeth as I spoke, "You still want me to come to that party?"

KAREN

"Hey, sweetie!" I smiled as my daughter burst through the front door of our small, rundown, farmhouse. I wished I could give her more every day, but there was no way John and I could afford any better. But she was happy, and that was all that mattered.

"Hey mom," she replied as she threw her backpack on the linoleum floor in the kitchen. She walked over to the refrigerator to grab something to eat.

"I think there's some leftover pasta in there if you're hungry. You missed dinner, so I put some in there for you," I said.

"Thanks, Mom. Yeah, sorry about that. I had to stay a little late for work. They needed some help with an elderly patient in cardiac arrest. He's doing fine now, thank God."

I smiled as my daughter recounted the events of her day. She had recently taken up an after school job as a nursing assistant at the local hospital. She had always wanted to become a nurse, and she had convinced John and me that this was the first step. I looked at the clock on the wall of the kitchen. It was eight-thirty p.m.

"How was school, Jennifer?" I asked her as she pulled the spaghetti out of the microwave.

She sat down next to me at the table and took a bite before answering. "It was all right. Boring as usual," she said. "But something great happened today! Remember how I told you about that guy at school?" I nodded as I listened to her story. "Well, he finally asked me to prom!"

I smiled at the joy that radiated off of her face as she spoke those words. "Honey, that's wonderful!" I replied. "How did he ask you?"

Jennifer smiled before recounting the events that led up to her moment of glory. "Well," she began. "He came up to me in the hallway and kneeled down in front of the entire school, holding out a single rose!"

I chuckled at her enthusiasm, remembering how easy life was for me back in high school. "A rose, for a dance at prom?" She laughed when she repeated his words, noting how cheesy they were, yet in the way she portrayed the event so excitedly, I could tell she loved how thoughtful his approach was.

I couldn't help but smile at my daughter, now all grown up. It felt like just yesterday she was born. I was holding a sweet, innocent baby in my arms—something so precious, so loving, so miraculous. I remember her thirteenth birthday when John and I had given her a cross necklace when she was old enough to make the decision to give her heart to God. She still wore it around her neck. Just barely four years later, and here she was, all of the wonderful individual I had expected her to be, and so much more to become.

CARLEY

I saw lights and heard music loud enough to burst my eardrums. I couldn't remember where I was, but none of that mattered. I took another shot from a bottle of tequila mixed with something else I had never heard of. I laughed for so long because I couldn't even remember what my name was, and it scared me. But in a twisted sort of way, I kind of liked not having control over myself. I liked the feeling of just doing whatever. But shortly after, that feeling was replaced with a nauseated one, and I found myself running from the crowd of people hovered around me and into the nearest bathroom. At least I thought it was a bathroom.

I fell to the cold, tile floor beneath me, grabbing whatever I could to catch whatever was about to come up. And then it happened. I vomited one...two...three times before wiping my face with the sleeve of my shirt. Then my eyes cleared up just enough for me to see that I was sitting in a laundry room, and I had thrown up into a box of kitty litter. "Oh well," I said to myself. "Easy cleanup."

I stood up shakily and stumbled to the door of the laundry room, only to plow right into Jason.

"Where've you been, C?" he asked.

"I'm just a little sick, but it's okay now." He nodded and grabbed my hand, leading me through the trashed house. Somehow, I found my way back into the crowd of people in the kitchen, who were cheering me on to the next shot. I had never been much of a sloppy drinker. I usually left that stuff to Jason, but everything going on with my mom was killing me. I just needed to be numb for a while.

KAREN

I heard footsteps behind me clomping down the stairs. I turned around to see Jennifer with her sweatshirt and night bag draped over her arms.

"Is it okay if I go to Natalie's tonight?" she asked.

I glanced again at the clock. Eleven thirty. "I don't know, Jen." I hesitated.

"Mom, please?" she begged. "I haven't seen Natalie in forever, and I've been working all night. I just need a little break."

I frowned at her. "All right, Jennifer, but you know I hate you driving this late."

"I know, Mom. Don't worry. I'm just going to Natalie's. I'll call you when I get there, okay?" she bargained.

"Don't forget," I warned.

"Okay. Thanks, Mom!" Jennifer yelled as she walked quickly toward the table to get her keys.

"Hey, Jen?" I whispered quietly.

"Yeah, Mom." She turned around to face me, her long brown hair flipping freely over her shoulders.

"Be careful, okay? I love you."

She walked slowly toward me and kissed me on the cheek. "I always am, Mom. I love you too." She smiled as she turned away. When she reached the door, I heard her pause and say, "I'll call you when I get there!" I turned back toward the computer screen in front of me as the door slammed shut behind her. A small tear welled up in my eye as I began to realize that soon Jennifer would be off to college, and my only child would be starting a brand new life without me. If anything was harder for a mom than letting go of her child, then it sure hadn't hit me yet. If it was that hard to let my daughter go to a friend's house, I couldn't imagine the day she left home next year.

"Calm down," I whispered to myself. "She'll always come back home." But something inside of me, yet I couldn't tell what it was, didn't quite believe that statement.

CARLEY

I fumbled with the keys of my new Mercedes Benz that I got last year for my birthday. Mom had it shipped to the house when she went to Cabo for the week with her boyfriend. I guess she thought the gift would make up for her not being there. I finally remembered I had a remote for my car. I clicked the button, liking the small sound it made in return. I pressed it again and again, finally realizing how out of it I really was.

My best friend, Britney, jumped into the seat beside me, and we tore out of the driveway, making our way down the road. Britney reached for the radio and turned up the volume so loud my head started spinning.

I glanced at the clock. Eleven forty-five. I laughed as I watched the speedometer climb from forty-five to fifty and then steadily up to eighty miles per hour. I didn't even feel the car speeding up, but I heard the wind whipping past my halfway-cracked window. It just became some sort of game to see how fast I could go.

It wasn't long before I was dancing and singing along to the music when I made the turn. I didn't know I was in the wrong lane.

The yellow lines on the road blurred together, so I didn't even know which side was the right side. The road was too small for me to tell. I didn't see the headlights coming. I swear I didn't.

KAREN

Something wasn't right that night. I felt it in my stomach. I took an antacid the doctor prescribed me for whenever I'm feeling so nervous that I need something to take off the edge.

It didn't help.

John was sitting in the living room watching ESPN with a can of Coke resting on the coffee table beside him. He was so calm. *How can he not feel what I'm feeling?* I asked myself. Maybe it was just a mother's intuition.

Although I couldn't explain it, I had to find out. I picked up the phone to call Jennifer, but then I hesitated, and eventually I set it back down. It had only been fifteen minutes since she left. Once she got to Natalie's, I knew she'd call. She promised.

So I sat at the kitchen table alone, waiting for the silent phone that rested in front of me to ring, easing my worries and my deepest fears that were climbing out from the depths of my soul and whispering in my ears.

CARLEY

The next thing I remembered was this loud, annoying screaming. It was about to burst my eardrums wide open. I felt like yelling at the stupid person to shut up...until I realized that the stupid person was me.

And then it hit me. The pain, it was unbearable, and it was searing through my entire body like nothing I had ever felt before. It felt like fire crawling over every part of my skin, and no matter how many times they poured water on, the fire would not go out. The worst pain was in my right leg.

I couldn't breathe. I was trying to suck in any air at all, and I started to panic. I was crying, and my eyes were so blurry I couldn't see anything around me. After a few minutes of endless pain and screaming, I finally realized I was at a hospital. I was being rushed into a small room, and soon I was parked right behind a curtain.

A few doctors were rushing around my bed, yelling unintelligible scientific terms to one another. I couldn't understand what they were saying. But the pain all over my body wouldn't let me ask any questions.

The only thing I could do was scream.

KAREN

John was sitting across from me at the kitchen table as I frantically dialed numbers on our phone. I called Natalie, and she said that Jennifer never got there. I called anywhere that she might have gone, and I even called all of her friends. The only places I hadn't called, for fear of knowing anything I wasn't ready to know, were the hospital and the police station. Those were last resort on a mother's list.

The thing that scared me the most was when I called Jennifer's phone; it went straight to voicemail. My heart began to panic when all of Jennifer's friends reported the same things.

"No, I haven't heard from her."

"Maybe her phone's dead, and she went to get gas or something." Those were the main explanations I had been given from her supportive and worried friends. I could hear the tension in their voices as they too feared the worst. I offered my thanks and apologized for calling so late, and then I set the phone down on the table.

John reached for my hand across the table, but I stood up before he could begin to comfort me. "I'm going to look for her," I said. I turned to grab my purse and keys from the coffee table in the living room.

"Now wait a minute—" John began. But before he could finish his sentence, the doorbell rang. The sound echoed through my ears as my heart pounded hard in my chest. John's startled eyes bored holes into mine. I shuddered under his scrutiny. I could feel him analyzing me. He knew what I was thinking, and he couldn't help but think the same.

"Sit down, Karen," he instructed.

I was never one to be bossed around before. I always had a strong sense of independence about myself for as long as I can remember, but the seriousness in my husband's voice scared me into cooperation.

I walked mechanically back to the kitchen table. John stood up slowly. The doorbell uttered yet another impatient cry.

I cringed.

My husband inched closer to the door and took hold of the handle, not bothering to peek through the window. He would know the truth soon enough.

Yet when the door finally cracked enough to reveal our guest clearly from where I sat, my heart completely sank. I gasped for air. My lungs were closing in on me. Every part of me was shutting down.

A lone policeman stood in front of my husband, whispering softly so only he could hear. I clasped my hand over my mouth, trying to calm myself down. The police officer stared at my husband with hard but compassionate eyes, as if he delivered this kind of news all the time.

Then John cried out in anguish and pain. It was a rush of emotions I had never heard come from him before. There was only one time I had seen him cry, and it was the day Jennifer was born.

I watched as the police officer uttered his sincerest apologies. I stood up from my chair, scraping it against the kitchen floor. This move attracted the attention of John and the policeman, who had been completely oblivious of my existence until this very moment.

John's eyes told me everything. "Oh God, no. No, no, please no!" I yelled.

The police officer looked away. I fell back into the chair, and my face collapsed into my hands. Muffled cries and a monsoon of tears surrounded me. John grabbed hold of me in his arms, and we cried. For what seemed like hours, we sat together holding onto anything that was left of who we once were, yet every time I looked up, the police officer was still standing at the doorway, his eyes on the floor—the one constant reminder that everything we had once known was about to change. John stood up after all of his tears had poured from his now red and puffy eyes. He brushed back my hair with his strong hands and looked deep into my eyes. I still had many more tears to shed, but managed to stifle them back as he turned to look at the ever-present police officer.

"Mr. and Mrs. Crawley, I know this is a difficult time for you both, but I am here to answer any questions you might have." His voice cracked uneasily as he fidgeted with the hat in his hand, but his eyes were laced with sympathy. Warmth projected from his posture, and I quickly nodded my head in response. I invited him into the kitchen to tell us the things no parent ever wants to be told but we needed to hear then, more than anything.

CARLEY

"What's going on?" I yelled to the nurses huddled over my bed. None of them would answer me as they checked clipboards and milled around, minding their own business. Soon a tall man with dark brown hair walked over to my bedside. He was dressed in blue scrubs with the dorkiest shoes on his feet.

I was surprised at the fact that I was in so much pain, yet I could still manage to scrutinize the outfit of the man before me.

He spoke in a powerful, yet soothing voice. "Carley," he began, "you've been in an accident."

This much I knew already. I had been having flashbacks ever since I arrived at the hospital. I remembered the music, the drinking, Britney and the radio, and then the lights.

Oh gosh, I remembered those lights. They stared at me head on, and I never felt so afraid. Even in my drunken stupor, I had realized that something was about to happen. And then, everything went black.

And there I was, lying in a hospital bed, in torturous pain, alone, with no one to tell me what was going on. The tall man above me introduced himself. "My name is Dr. Dale, and I am assigned to be your doctor during your stay here at the hospital. I will be available if you have any questions, so please feel free to ask." I thought quietly to myself, *Well, you haven't been too eager to answer the questions I had earlier.*

I watched his face intently as he quickly scanned the clipboard in his hand. "We've called your mother, and she will try to get in as quickly as she can. She said she's a little ways away right now and to let you know she'll catch the quickest plane back to the city."

This news stunned me. "Out of the city?" I asked. "She's out of the city?"

Dr. Dale looked at me quizzically, with his Harry Potter glasses propped up low on the bridge of his nose. "You didn't know?" he asked.

"Of course I didn't know. I wouldn't have asked you if I'd known!" I spat.

"Well, sounds to me like you have a personal problem on your hands. Let me know if you need another dose of painkillers. I'll send in a nurse to re-administer," he said as he began to walk out of the hospital room.

"Now! Now!" I yelled at him. "I need the stuff now!"

With a flick of his wrist, he waved good-bye. Anger, like I'd never before experienced, boiled to the surface and spread throughout my pain-filled body. I slammed my head back onto the pillow. "So much for the help, doc," I whispered to myself. "You really answered a lot of my questions."

"Don't take it personal, sweetheart," a soft voice spoke at the entrance of the room. "The doctor has a busy schedule. He does everything he can for as many people as possible."

I looked up to see an old nurse with almost-gray hair readjusting my pillow behind my head. "Will you please help me?" I asked pathetically.

"Of course, sweetie. That's kind of my job." She chuckled. "What can I get you?" she asked as she administered more painkillers.

"Please tell me what happened. And is Britney okay?"

The nurse looked at me sympathetically. "Well, you were in a very bad automobile accident. You and your friend had been drinking a lot, earlier last night when you started driving. An older man found your car and the other while driving home to his house. You had wrecked with another car while coming around the curb. You were going seventy miles per hour. Thank God you hit head on, because if you had just barely clipped it, it could've sent you flipping.

"You received a pretty nasty broken leg from the accident, and you'll probably be prepped for surgery tomorrow. We have to wait for your mother to get here first to sign the papers. You also had a collapsed lung, a broken wrist, and a nasty concussion. We operated on the lung last night, part of emergency surgery." I quickly interjected, "But what about Britney?" The nurse paused for a second before giving me any more feedback, almost as if weighing her options of whether or not to tell me what happened.

"Now your friend, well she's doing fine. She's had surgery on her left arm, and she has a pretty bad concussion as well. She's awfully bruised, as both of you are, but she'll be just fine once she heals, and thank God, so will you."

A sigh of relief swept through me, but soon, an awful feeling ruptured inside my soul. "What about the other car?" I asked. The picture of the lights burst into my brain once again, reminding me that something terrible was about to happen.

The nurse stared at me for a while before speaking. "I probably should wait until your mother arrives."

That statement confirmed what I knew was already true. Emotion swept through me as I realized what I had done. "I…I killed someone?" I trembled, and I could feel my body growing intensely hot as another burst of pain ripped through me.

"Sweetheart, it really is no one's fault. Sometimes these things just happen. It was bad judgment, that's all." She forced a weak smile.

My face, still twisted with pain, and now shock, stared directly at her. "I killed someone?" I repeated.

"Let's wait until your mom gets here, please."

She stood up to walk away, but I called out to beg her to stay. "Please! No, come back! I have to know. Please, can you tell me who it was?" Half of me begged her to turn around and walk away, as if never knowing the name of the victim would make it less real.

Instead, she pulled up one of the stools sitting on the other side of the room and inched closer to my bedside. "Listen, what I'm about to tell you, well, understand I'm not allowed to say anything to you regarding this situation until your mother arrives."

I nodded my head, understanding that this woman was risking her job to tell me something she would want to know if she was in my position.

"Last night, a teenage girl went to go stay at a friend's house. She left her house around the same time you left your party. Both of you hit one another coming around the curve at Camillo's bend. The girl was almost eighteen, and she was killed instantly. Her name was Jennifer Crawley."

My heart stopped. My eyes began to blur and black out as I realized the full effects of my dangerous joyride.

"Did you know her?" the nurse asked me.

I took a deep, shuddering breath before I answered, "Yes. I knew her." And then, I began to cry.

The nurse wrapped her arms around me, whispering, "Oh, honey, it's all right. I understand how hard it is to lose a friend."

Even though this woman was sweet, she didn't understand the reason why I was crying. The truth is, I never was friends with Jennifer. In fact, I could never stand her. She always acted so much better than everyone else. Just because she carried around a Bible all day long didn't make her better than the rest of us. But to tell the truth, I was jealous. At times, I even wished I had something to believe in, and I had come close to believing in God quite a few times. Yet every time the opportunity presented itself, something would always happen that would make me second-guess my decision. Oftentimes, something my mom would say or do would make me doubt that God was even out there, let alone that he cared about someone like me. Now that he had let this happen to Jennifer, it made me sure that there was no way he loved me. If he could do this to Jennifer, the one girl who never stopped believing in him, then what would he do to me?

I'd always thought I was a good person, someone who was always nice to everyone; but now, as tears poured down my cheeks, I realized that last night I did the one thing to Jennifer, and her family, that I could never take back.

KAREN

I was sitting in my daughter's room. Jennifer's room. It was a mess. I remembered back to the day before she died. I had asked her to clean up a little before she left for school. I was so appreciative of her disobedience for this very reason. It felt like she was still with me. Everything felt the same. I might sound crazy, but I even took out some of her clothes from her dresser and threw them onto the floor. I was sitting in the midst of T-shirts and jeans, missing the young girl who's supposed to be wearing them.

I couldn't help but cry. I just couldn't stop. I was dying inside. Everything was gone, and I couldn't do it anymore.

My only daughter had been taken away from me, and she was never coming back.

I found one of Jennifer's jackets and wrapped it around my shivering shoulders. I crawled into her unmade bed, pulling the sheets high up over my head. I lay down on the same pillow that Jen rested her head on just two nights before. And I started to cry. In fact, I don't think I've stopped since I got the news.

John had been trying to comfort me, suggesting that we see a Christian grief counselor. But I just couldn't do it that soon. Because if I decided to see a counselor, that meant I was ready to face the pain. It meant I was ready to come to terms with what happened. It meant that I was ready to let go of my daughter, and I just couldn't do that.

t was almost three hours since I stumbled my way into Jennifer's room. I had fallen asleep on her bed, and I had just awoken to the sound of mumbling voices downstairs. I quietly crept down the hall and toward the top of the stairs. The voices grew louder.

I heard my husband talking quietly to someone. And then I heard the guest's voice. Jennifer! I clumsily fumbled my way down the stairs, and I ran to my little girl sitting at the table in front of me. I wrapped my arms around her, heaving uncontrollably.

"I knew you weren't gone!" I yelled. "I knew God still had plans for you!" I laughed to myself, pulling Jennifer as close to me as possible. I looked over to see John's face, horrified.

"John." I smiled. "Don't look so afraid! Jenny's back!" I calmly patted Jennifer's head, playing with the spirally curls that were winding around her small-framed face.

And then I remembered. Jennifer had straight hair.

I looked down. In the place of where my daughter had been just moments before, sat my sister, Annabelle, wearing the most shocked expression.

I wanted to slap myself. I could only imagine how crazy I looked to my husband and sister right then.

"Oh no," I cried. "Oh no, no, no! How could I be this stupid?"

Annabelle stood up to wrap me in a warm embrace, her tears soaking into the shoulder of the sweater I was wearing.

John put his head in his hands and wept. I stood there in awe, watching my husband suffer through one of the hardest trials we would ever have to face. Annabelle held me close to her, and the tears came. They poured from my eyes, and my heart sank. *Jennifer is gone,* I told myself. *She's never coming back.* No matter how many times I said that, I didn't believe it. I couldn't.

CARLEY

I was sitting in my hospital room, eyeing my mother, who was plopped in the corner chair by the wall. "Where were you?" I asked.

"You are not the one who is allowed to ask questions. What the heck were you thinking, Carley?"

I flinched at her harsh words.

"I mean, I just can't understand what would possess you to get in the car completely drunk. I mean, I knew you were stupid…just not that stupid."

My ears began to close at the sound of that word. "I am *not* stupid!" I yelled. "And don't ever call me that again!" Tears sprang to my eyes as a look of surprise rushed over my mom's face.

She stood steadily from her chair. "What I meant is that sometimes the decisions you make are stupid." She paused. "Carley, I don't think you understand what you've done. There are so many things you're going to have to go through in these next couple months. I would get prepared if I were you. I have to go. I'll be back later tonight."

I watched my mom walk out the door and then get stopped by my new nurse friend waiting at the entrance. She quickly signed the papers for my surgery and left, not a trace of sympathy or care in her wake.

The nurse walked into my room smiling. "Busy woman, huh?" she asked. "Always," I replied.

"Well, sometimes that's just how it is. You're lucky she can support you. I'm struggling enough as it is, raising three grandkids on this salary. It's tough. You're very blessed, I'll tell you that."

I looked at her thoughtfully. "You know, you've been such a help to me, and I don't even know your name."

The nurse laughed. "Oh, well, silly me! You know, when you get to be my age, you forget the simplest introductory procedures. Let's start over, shall we?"

I nodded.

"Good evening, your majesty, my name is Dolores, and I will be at your service during your stay."

I laughed, but quickly stopped after a sharp pain shot through my leg. "Well, thank you for your service, kind lady. I will need all the medicinal power you possess to get me through the rest of my stay."

She took the hint and gave me a small pill for the pain. She helped hold up my head as I swallowed and then lay back on the pillow.

"Well, madam, I hate to break the news, but your court awaits you. In other words, we're going to have to begin prepping for surgery."

I groaned, nauseated from the pain meds and now the smell of sterile equipment around me. But even through all of this pain and sickness, I still couldn't stop thinking about Jennifer.

KAREN

I gently picked up the phone. I had to know who it was. I had to know who took Jennifer away from me.

I called the policeman who was at our door. As hard as it was to believe, when we were sitting in the kitchen with him, the night of the accident, we never asked the question about who did it. It never crossed our minds. But lately, it had been nagging at me.

The long, black dress that enveloped me was itchy and tattered. It was nothing that resembled my beautiful daughter. I walked to the bathroom carrying the phone so my husband wouldn't come in and hear me. He was waiting in the car, getting ready to drive to the church for Jennifer's funeral.

Finally, Officer O'Neal picked up. "Hello," he answered. I sucked in a deep breath before saying, "Hello, yes, David…"

I made my way out to the car parked in my driveway. John sat in the front seat, tapping his fingers on the steering wheel impatiently. I climbed quietly into the car and put on my seatbelt. I stared blankly ahead as John slid his fingers over to my side of the car to grab my hand. I sat there, too shocked to move a muscle.

"Karen, this is not something I want to do either. But I want you to know that even though this is the hardest thing we will ever do, I will always be right here," John whispered.

I turned to look at him, a flash of sympathy flooding my eyes. Yet it was still mixed in with the despair I felt just minutes before on the phone with Officer O'Neal.

John first picked up the sadness in my expression. "What's wrong Karen?" he questioned, a look of worry and panic in his eyes. "I talked to David," I said.

"What did he say?" John's voice grew raspier, more intense, as if one more drop of bad news would send him spiraling into the pit of despair, severing every last tie we had left with reality.

"He wouldn't say who it was, but we will find out in court when we appear for the trial."

John sighed and looked urgently out the window. "I have to know who killed her." John's head lowered and I heard him sniffle. He put the car into reverse, and we backed out of the driveway.

CARLEY

"The funeral was today," my mom whispered as she sat next to my bed. I was still drowsy from the anesthesia they had used to make me sleep for surgery.

"What?" I managed to utter from my dry, chapped lips.

"Jennifer's funeral. It was today," she replied calmly and with a hint of guilt in her voice.

My eyes followed her blonde hair resting neatly on her shoulders. I sighed, feeling a complete rush of sadness. Not just for the fact that I had done something I would regret for the rest of my life, but the fact that when I looked at my mom, I realized something terrible. The woman sitting in front of me was no longer my mom. We had abandoned all hope of ever being okay again the day she decided not to care anymore. The pretty, blonde lady who sat in front of me was now a stranger.

I closed my eyes, giving her the hint. I listened as she stood up and made her way to the door. But before the door closed on its normal four second interval between opening it, I heard the stranger sigh. And I could feel her eyes on me. I was uncertain of what this meant. I listened even more intently. A few more seconds went by without any sound, and I thought she had gone, but the door had never closed.

Then another sigh escaped her mouth. I heard her turn and shut the door. She was disappointed. I could tell that much. She was tired of the way I acted, the careless attitude I always portrayed.

But she didn't understand I was disappointed too. Disappointed with the late nights alone at home, without anyone to talk to. The secret weekend getaways when she wouldn't even say good-bye before leaving. I was disappointed in her as a mother and as a decent human being.

I glanced around my room for the first time since I had arrived. Plain, white walls surrounded me as well as medicinal cabinets hammered onto them. A small sink rested across from my bed, and the other, empty bed next to mine sat lonely in its place.

Alone.

That was the one word that described everything now. That bed was alone. I was alone, mom was alone, and I had even left Jennifer's parents alone. I had taken away the one thing in their life that they lived for. If I had done that, what would become of them? What would become of me?

I rested my head back on the pillow. Alone.

KAREN

The second I got home, I jumped out of that awful black dress and threw it in the trashcan outside. I couldn't ever touch that disgusting thing again.

I was drowning; gasping for air, but nobody was reaching out to help me.

I couldn't do it anymore. I'd spent my whole life praying. I prayed to a God who was known to be merciful, loving, and dependable. But then, all I could think of when I prayed was how God took my daughter away from me.

All I kept seeing was them lowering that black casket into the ground.

My stomach wretched when I thought of Jennifer in that box. My daughter was buried in the ground. She was too young for that. John held me steady as my knees grew weak. I wanted to die. There was no reason to live anymore. Jennifer was gone. Everything was gone. I would never see her again, and Carley was still alive. I felt hate toward Carley, so much hate, and it was eating me alive. But I would have rather felt this hate any day than forgive her. I couldn't do that. I would not ever forgive her. I wanted her to feel what I was feeling, and if I forgave her, then she never would.

I ran straight up the stairs into Jennifer's room and climbed into her bed. I heard John walk solemnly from the living room and shut the door to our bedroom. I heard his muffled cries escaping from the room across the hall. Just hearing my strong husband cry like an infant ripped every ounce of hope from my heart.

I had no hope any longer. Jennifer took that with her the night she said good-bye.

CARLEY

Rain pattered softly on the window by my bedside. I got to see Britney for the first time since the accident. Dolores got me a wheelchair from the supply closet, and I was able to wheel myself into her room. I hesitated at the door, afraid to find out if anything had changed between us. A rush of relief swept across me as I opened the door and saw an energetic Britney lying in a hospital bed.

When she saw me, a look of horror stretched across her delicate face. Then, I saw them. Her family. Britney's mom, dad, and older brother sat in uncomfortable hospital chairs in the corner. They all had smiles plastered on their faces, but they quickly disappeared once they saw me at the door.

I contemplated turning back and leaving, pretending like I never even went in there. But it was too late. I looked down at the floor, embarrassed at my boldness to intrude in my best friend's life, in more ways than one.

"What do you want?" Britney's mom callously whispered. I cringed at the venom in her words. She might as well have spat fire in my face. I watched as Britney's dad rested his hand on her quivering arm, as if to contain any volatile outbursts. I watched her take a deep breath, inviting just the tiniest hint of calm into her flaring nostrils.

I sat there quietly, not responding. I looked up at Britney for some help, but her menacing glare bored holes through my shattered heart. That's just like Britney. She was always a copycat of her malicious mom.

I can't believe it took me this long to finally realize that we were never really friends at all. If the person you call your best friend can drop you as easy as that, then they aren't a real friend.

"I think you should leave." I stared at Britney in disbelief as she hissed that awful sentence to me. Her brother wiggled uncomfortably in his chair, obviously noticing the thick tension in the room.

I looked toward Britney's dad and saw a flash of sympathy pass through his eyes. "We really aren't encouraging visitors right now. Maybe you should come back another time."

I nodded feverishly and spun the wheelchair around to face the door. Before I could get halfway out the door, I managed to hear Britney's mom whisper, a little too loud, "…all her fault."

Tears poured down my face as I wheeled myself into the hallway. I rushed back to my room and hoisted myself up into the bed using the wrist straps the nurse had given me. Grabbing the covers and yanking them over my head, I cried.

I cried for Jennifer. I cried for her family. I cried for my mom and for my best friend. I had ruined so many lives, including mine.

And I could never, ever take it back.

KAREN

It had been almost three days since the funeral. I hadn't come out of Jennifer's room. I didn't know what I was doing by locking myself up in there, but I just couldn't face anything else. John had been bringing up food every day and opening the door just to check on me. I hadn't said one word to him, but I hoped he understood. It wasn't because I didn't love him. God knows it wasn't that. But he didn't understand what I was going through. Nobody did. I looked around Jenny's room, staring extra long at anything and everything that reminded me of her. And I started to cry.

I was crying so loudly that when the door cracked open, I didn't even hear. Then, I felt John's arms around me, somehow weaker than before.

His touch startled me, and I jumped, more out of bottled anger than out of surprise. "Stop!" I yelled. "Get away from me! Don't ever talk to me again!"

I turned away from him, knowing that my words had been like a dagger to his heart. His ragged breathing slowly calmed. He stood and walked back to the door.

Before he turned around to shut it, I heard him whisper, "You're not the only one who lost someone, Karen."

His words sent chills up and down my back. I shivered there on the floor of my daughter's bedroom. I turned around, only to see an empty hallway.

CARLEY

All I could think about was Jennifer—how jealous I was of her and what happened on that awful night. I kept hearing the music and seeing the headlights. And the worst part is, I kept hearing the sound of twisting metal. I cringe every time.

I couldn't feel alive again because Jennifer was dead.

It wasn't long before a knock at my hospital room door startled me from my depressing thoughts. I eagerly lifted my eyes to the visitor standing across from me. Elation soared through my body, and I cried out in happiness and surprise. "Jason!"

He smiled as he rushed to my bedside. I hadn't seen him since the night of the accident, but the nurses told me he had come by a few times when I was sleeping. We embraced, and in that moment, I felt safe again. I felt love and hope. I felt alive.

All of a sudden, a rush of emotions from the past events overwhelmed me. A flood of tears began pouring from my eyes as I cried into my boyfriend's shoulder. A wonderful moment of reuniting and happiness had turned into something so grievous and heart wrenching. I cried louder and louder as Jason held me there in his arms.

"Why?" I yelled. "Why did this happen to me?"

Jason hugged me tighter, not saying a word. He rested his chin on the top of my head, and I just sat there, for what seemed like an eternity, crying like the baby I wish I was again.

"I'm sorry, Carley. I'm so sorry this happened to you. I'm so sorry," Jason whispered calmly into my ear. His words were comforting, but I still couldn't shake that awful feeling inside of me that constantly reminded me of what I'd done.

After a while, when I had cried out everything left in me, I slowly pulled away from Jason's strong embrace. He lovingly reached up to my face and brushed away a tear that was running down my cheek.

"I don't know why this happened to you, Carley, but I want you to know one thing. Please don't blame yourself for this. If you need to blame anyone, then blame me. It was my fault. I shouldn't have made you come to the party."

Jason's eyes lowered to the ground as he sat there holding my hand.

I tugged at his shirt sleeve, forcing him to look at me once again. "Please don't say that," I whispered. "It was never your fault. It's always been mine."

He pulled my hand up to his lips, kissed my palm, and sat there holding his face to my hand.

And then he started to cry.

Shock overwhelmed me. I had never seen Jason cry before. He held my hand over his face, not willing to show me this new, sensitive side of him. I pulled my hand away to look at him.

He quickly stood up from his seat and walked toward the window, staring intently at nothing. Then he turned around to look at me, intense sorrow burning in his eyes. "When I got the call from Britney's mom, of course, she thought you'd need someone with you. Since your mom was gone, I was next in line. I can't explain to you how I felt. It was like something had been ripped out of me. It was the worst feeling I've ever felt in my life, Carley. I thought you were dead. I thought I would never see you again."

He paused to collect himself, but his strength was no match for the raw emotion surrounding him at this moment. "I stayed with you the first night. I don't know if you remember, but you had so many surgeries that night. You were so close to leaving me, C."

Tears poured from his eyes as he sat down beside me again. "I didn't know it then, but I sure do now. I can't live without you, Carley. I just can't do it. I came too close to losing you that night, so I had to leave. I had to think about a few things. I wanted to be the first one you saw when you woke up, but I couldn't stay. I hope you understand."

I nodded compassionately, grateful to see, no matter how selfish, someone else suffering along with me.

"Carley, I don't ever want to lose you." Jason kissed my hand lightly.

I smiled at him. "You won't," I replied. Then, a sharp knock on the door startled me from my gaze.

Before I could answer, a tall woman with a navy blue pant-suit walked briskly into my room. She held a square, black, briefcase, and her hair was pinned back into a neat bun. She had wire-rimmed glasses that framed her square face. "Good morning, Carley. My name is Heather Stone, and I will be your attorney. Your mother hired me."

She never even looked me in the eye. She pulled out so many papers from her briefcase, shoving them aside, and then rearranged them again.

"My attorney?" I asked.

"Yes, I'm your attorney. I will be representing you in court."

My heart stopped. Jason's grip on my hand tightened. Of course I had known I would be punished. There was no way I could get away from this mess I had created. But it was just so soon, and I was afraid.

KAREN

I finally stood up from Jennifer's floor and worked up enough courage to take a shower and fix myself something to eat. I walked downstairs and headed for the kitchen. I was surprised to see John sitting at the table with a box of pictures and things spread out in front of him. When I got closer, I realized it was the box Jennifer had kept under lock and key. It contained some of her most valuable possessions, such as pictures of her and her friends, her favorite CD's, and most importantly, her prayer journal.

Jennifer had always kept her prayer journal with her ever since she was little. John and I gave it to her when she was ten years old. She used to curl up on the couch every day after school to talk to God about her day. John and I watched in amazement as our little girl grew so quickly into a strong young woman with a thrill and zest for God. She was all that we could've asked for.

I walked slowly toward the table and looked at John. It was the first time he had seen me outside of Jen's room for nearly a week.

I felt awkward as I waited for him to speak, like it was the first day of elementary school, and all I wanted to do was find acceptance and friendship.

I breathed a sigh of relief as John looked up and smiled at me. Although he looked tired and completely overwhelmed, he had smiled nonetheless, and that was the first ray of sunshine I'd seen in this awful storm.

He motioned to the chair beside him, offering me a seat. I sat down and ran my hands across the pictures scattered on the table. I remember some of them. Jennifer with her youth group on their mission trip to Africa. Another with her and her father at the zoo by the penguin cage. And a very special one that she kept from Christmas two years ago. It was the Christmas she got her first pet puppy, Cooper. He was just a little white ball of fluff back then. I smiled at the memory.

I continued to look around at the pictures, but the one thing that really pulled at my attention was Jennifer's prayer journal. I must have been obvious when I glanced over at it because I heard John say, "Go ahead, I was saving it for you to read first anyway."

I smiled weakly, reaching across the table and grabbing the big, yellow journal covered in doodles and pictures. I carefully flipped it open to the first page.

"Before you read it," John said, "I want to let you know I found out who caused the accident. One of Jennifer's friends at the hospital told me they had another car accident victim. Her name is Carley Jameson, and she went to school with Jennifer."

I nodded my head solemnly, having anticipated this moment for so long, wanting to know who took Jennifer away from me, only to find that the answer did not heal my aching heart. I turned my attention back to the journal, forgetting everything of the past and focusing on what was still in my control.

A few of her first entries had been ripped out, but I didn't care. I would look for them later. My eyes eagerly skimmed over the paper, familiarizing myself with Jennifer's handwriting. It read,

Dear God,

Today was really draining. I am so tired now because of everything. I tried to witness to people in my English class by reading a book in the Bible as my book report. Unfortunately, it didn't go as I planned. When I was in the middle of my book report, my teacher yelled at me for bringing church into school, and all of the kids just sat there. Lord, today was supposed to be such a good day. I knew that I would've gotten so many people to follow you, but it just didn't work out that way. I remember Pastor Dave saying something about never abandoning you. He said that we should always stand up for what we believe in, no matter what. Because in the end, that's all that really matters. And that's what Jesus did. He went through so much pain and hurt just to prove to everyone that he would not give up on you. So that's what I did. I told my teacher that I was going to finish my book report and then I would sit down. She didn't say anything. So I started presenting again. And this time, people listened. When I was finished, the *whole class started clapping and three people, including my teacher, came up to me after class and asked me how to have a relationship with you. Lord, I want to give you all the thanks in the world! You have shown me so much love and mercy, and I can't thank you enough for giving me the strength to stand up to my teacher. I'm happy to be your daughter. Please continue to give me strength, Lord. In your Son's name I pray,*

amen.

Anger surfaced in me after I set the book down. Jennifer was the daughter I had always wanted, and so much more. She was perfect. After reading this entry, Jennifer had surprised and astounded me at her steadfastness to God. It was then that I realized what a special girl she was, and how much I wished to be like her.

I stood up from the table and walked quickly to the sink. I ran the cold water from the faucet and splashed it on my face. After a few minutes, I turned off the water and grasped the edges of the sink.

"I hate her!" I yelled.

John turned around immediately, stunned by the rage in my voice. All he did was watch.

"I hate Carley!" I repeated. "I hate what she did to us! And what she did to Jennifer!" I slammed my fist down on the counter. John stared, waiting patiently for me to calm down.

Soon after my outburst, my rage left me, and I leaned up against the counter, still maintaining eye contact with my all-too-quiet husband. "Why don't you hate her?" I asked, all intensity and boldness now gone from my voice. I sat there, helpless and weak, begging him to contradict the question I had just aimed his way. I was eager to hear him say that he did, in fact, hate Carley as much as I did.

But he let me down, or I let myself down, I guess you could say.

"Why are you letting her get away with this?" I asked.

John stood up and walked toward me. He pulled me into his strong arms, and I just fell apart. But in the midst of all the tears and the muffled screams, I could make out every word John whispered in my ears. "I'm forgiving her because Jennifer would want that. Jennifer would want us to be happy. You are only hurting yourself by not forgiving her."

I pulled away from his embrace. "You really believe that?" I asked.

"Yes, Karen, I do."

I looked down at my feet, now aware of the seriousness in his voice. That same seriousness I had overlooked on numerous accounts, but it was now too strong to ignore.

I worked up the courage to look my husband in the eyes. His weak smile provided the littlest bit of comfort. I went back into his arms and wept.

CARLEY

It should have been a good day. I was finally well enough to go home, but instead a cop was standing outside of my door waiting for me to get dressed.

Tears were pouring from my eyes as I packed up my things. My mom and Jason were running around the hospital room trying to pack up everything from toothbrushes and clothes to teddy bears and get-well cards. Once everything was loaded up in the car, Jason drove to my house to drop off all of my things before going back to school.

He missed too many school days because of me. The counselor told him that if he didn't come back and finish the year, then he would lose his football scholarship. It was all I could do to get him to go back.

But before he jumped in his car, he walked over to me and wrapped me in a tight embrace. "You're one of the strongest people I know, C. You're going to get through this...*We're* going to get through this."

A few tears escaped my eyes and dotted his dark gray T-shirt. I pulled away after the cop cleared his throat impatiently. "Bye Jay," I whispered. I turned to walk away, but he called out to me. "Don't forget! One of the strongest people I know."

I tried to muster a smile, but fear overpowered my emotions, and I could barely even bring myself to wave good-bye as the cop held the back door open for me. My mom waved from the corner as I climbed into the car.

We pulled up to the detention center where I was processed and given a change of clothes. I wasn't allowed to have anything with me. The officers led me into a small cell where I waited barely twenty minutes before being pulled out and escorted to a room with wooden planks for walls. It was a courtroom. Pews were lined up from the back of the room, all the way up to the stands. I had only seen courtrooms on TV before, but I had never felt like this. Fear pulsed through my veins. This wasn't a TV show. This was my life.

I looked at the empty room. Well, it was almost empty. My mother sat in the pew closest to the front. Her hair was a mess, so unlike my mother. The collar of her shirt was untucked, and it popped up at a weird angle. Obviously unbeknownst to her, she had two different earrings on. I had never seen my mother look that disheveled.

What had become of her? What had become of us?

The officer led me to a small table sitting before the judge's seat. Then the doors opened, and I saw Heather Stone, my attorney, enter the quiet room. She took her seat beside me and opened her briefcase.

She looked at me and said, "Carley, do you know why you're here?"

I stared at her with tear-filled eyes. It was too much for me to handle right then.

I shook my head, afraid that if I spoke, the tears would come.

"This is your arraignment. This is where we will establish myself as your attorney, and bond will be set for you."

Her words glided through my head. I didn't understand any of it. It felt like my brain had gone to mush. I turned to face the front of the room just in time to see a large man emerge from a doorway in the wooden wall. He wore a black robe, and it was easy to determine him as the judge. I had seen enough Law & Order to know that much.

"All rise!" the officer at the stand roared.

My mother, Heather, and I all stood up from our seats.

"You may be seated…" The officer went on to deliver his introductory speech as I waited in absolute agony. My heartbeat grew faster and faster as I realized how serious my situation was.

As soon as the officer stopped talking, the judge began. "Carley Jameson,

I've taken a look at your record and am sad to say it is far from perfect."

I lowered my head, knowing that the worst was yet to come.

"I see that you have had one previous DUI. You've been charged with possession of an illegal substance and shoplifting on numerous occasions." He set down the stack of papers he had been reading from and pushed his glasses higher up on the bridge of his nose. His thick, grey mustache fluttered every time he breathed. The judge looked up at me with convicting eyes.

I shivered.

"Carley, I don't know who you are, and I sure don't know anything about you, but judging from your previous record, you're screwing up your life."

I glared at him, a fire blazing within me.

"Looks to me like you need to get your act together."

Anger pulsed through me, and it was all I could do not to yell at this annoying man sitting lazily in front of me, telling me what I needed to do with *my* life.

"So I'm assuming that you're her attorney, Mrs. Stone?" the judge stated.

"Yes, Your Honor, I will be representing Carley Jameson in court," Heather replied.

The judge stared at me for a second before standing up from his seat. "Well, good luck. Including your previous encounters with the law, I'm setting your bond, Miss Jameson, at ten thousand dollars. You will receive notice on the details of your next court date." He pounded the gavel on the stand and walked off.

"All rise!" the officer called again. The three people in the room stood up until the judge left the room. The officer walked back over to me, placing handcuffs on my wrists once again. I watched as my mom stood up and walked toward me. "I'm going to pay your bail. You'll be out in about an hour." She turned and walked briskly away, and it was then I realized that my mother was wearing sandals and one sock with her business suit.

KAREN

I got a call from the county telling me that John and I would need to appear in court with Carley toward the end of the month. This court date would decide her fate. I felt a thrill knowing that whatever I said could change Carley's life forever. In a sick sort of way, I liked it. I almost wanted to stand up in front of the judge on that day and just convict her. I wanted to stand in front of Carley and explain how she ripped my heart out of me. I wanted to show everyone in that court room that Carley Jameson killed my daughter.

After I hung up the phone, I walked into the kitchen, where I found John sitting at the table with a turkey sandwich in his hands. He set it down on his plate when I walked in. I took a seat beside him and told him about the call.

His tired eyes grew even darker as I told him that soon we would need to testify in Carley's sentencing trial. I could understand why his mood darkened. This approaching court date would not bring us justice. It would not bring Carley back. It would only open up the wounds that we had worked so hard to heal. It would only rip apart the fragile seams we had miraculously sewed back together.

I reached across the table and grabbed his hand. I held it for a while. John gradually lifted his eyes to look at me. A tired smile stretched across his face, and I took it in. In that smile, I saw something. I saw Jennifer. Our family and friends had always said that Jennifer looked exactly like me, but for the first time, I saw her smile on John's face.

Tears formed behind my eyes, and I had to turn away before they began to pour. John squeezed my hand, and at that moment I knew what I had to do.

I had to forgive Carley Jameson, not for myself, but for Jennifer.

CARLEY

It had been almost a month since my arraignment. Mom kept her word, and in less than an hour, I was back in our car, heading home.

I hadn't spoken to my mother since the arraignment. She hadn't even been home. She left notes around the house telling me where she is. Sometimes she was meeting with the attorney, preparing for my next court date, and other times she was out with her friends, flying to Vegas. I don't think I had ever been that alone before.

Jason tried to help me cope with everything, but sometimes I just needed some space. Every time I tried to push him away, he'd complain, "You need me, C. Don't keep me in the dark."

I hated it when he said that, because honestly, I didn't need anyone. Nobody ever really truly cared. Nobody. And if that's the way it had to be, then why should I waste my time caring about anyone else?

When I walked down the stairs this morning to find something to eat, the phone rang. I picked it up. "Hello?" I said.

"Carley, it's me." My mother. "I just talked to Heather, and your court date has been scheduled for this Wednesday at eleven thirty."

My heart skipped a beat. "Okay. Thanks for telling me." The phone went dead after my mother hung up.

I shrunk down to the floor and sat there. I hugged my knees close to my chest, and I cried. The day where my whole future would be decided was only two days away. The family I had ruined would be there too, probably yelling and crying and begging the judge to have pity on them. How can I blame them? I would do the same thing. I had shredded Jennifer's family apart. And it would never be okay.

KAREN

"I don't think I can do this, God," I prayed. I kneeled down beside my bed, resting my elbows on my mattress. "I'm afraid to forgive her. I'm afraid that I'm betraying Jennifer by doing this. I don't know why this is so hard, God." Tears began pouring down my face. "She was my baby. My sweet, little baby. And now she's gone, and you expect me to just be okay with that?"

My words were so muffled as I cried that I was startled when my husband said in response, "Yes. You *have* to be okay with it. You have to understand that Jennifer is gone. You have to realize that holding hatred in your heart will never bring her back."

I turned around slowly to face him standing alone in the doorway. "You make it sound so easy," I said.

"Karen, this kind of thing is never easy. It will remain a struggle every day of our lives. But we have to overcome. If we don't, then we'll become prisoners of hate, and Jennifer would be so disappointed in us."

John knelt down beside me and closed his eyes.

"Dear Lord, please give us strength to take this day one step at a time. Today will be one of the hardest days of our lives. I know it will bring back so many raw emotions that we've fought so hard to hide, but Lord, please let all of our pain and sadness bring us closer to you. Help rid us of these awful feelings of hatred and hurt, so we can be filled with your love and peace once again. Lord, we know nothing will ever be the same, but we hope you will heal our hearts. Lord, please be with Carley and her family on this day, as it is a turning point in their lives, as well as ours. Sometimes we don't understand why these things happen, but you've promised that in time, we will know. Lord, we thank you for this day, and we thank you for each other. Tell Jennifer we love her and we miss her, and we can't wait to see her again one day. In your Son's name we pray, amen."

I raised my head to look at my husband, who now looked so much stronger than I'd ever seen him. He offered me his hand, and we stood up together. We walked out of the bedroom and to the car.

We were on our way to court, to forgive the little girl who needed forgiveness the most.

CARLEY

I just couldn't stop shaking. Fear was reverberating off the walls around me. I felt like I couldn't breathe as I walked mechanically down the hall with my mom and Heather. Jason was holding on tightly to my arm. He'd been great, he really had. I couldn't have asked for anyone more supportive.

As we reached the door to the courtroom, I heard someone calling my name. "Carley!"

I turned my head around to face the couple quickly approaching me. The woman was tall with dark brown hair flowing freely around her face. Her husband was tall as well, with glasses and dark, grey-speckled hair. When they got close enough for me to recognize them, it was too late to run.

Panic exploded inside of my stomach, and I felt like I was going to get sick. There was no air in my lungs, and everything started to spin. I looked into the eyes of this woman standing nearly two feet away from me, and I saw her—Jennifer. She was right there. Her eyes, her hair, everything. She was staring at me with a loving and warm smile, and I started to calm down. In fact, I had never felt more calm. I smiled back, even though just seconds ago I was about to pass out.

Then, Jennifer's mother spoke, "If we could just have a few minutes, we would really like to talk to you alone. I promise, we won't be long." Jennifer's mom looked toward my mother, seeking permission.

My mom hesitated but then nodded slowly. She motioned to Jason and Heather, and they stepped into the courtroom to prepare.

Jennifer's parents led me over to a small bench sitting in the hallway. Her mother sat in between her husband and me. I jumped out of surprise when she reached out and took my hand. I had nothing to say.

"Carley…" she began. "I love Jennifer, with all my heart. We both do." She motioned to her husband.

I nodded.

"And sometimes when you love someone, you don't ever want to let them go."

Tears began to surface as I started to notice the pain in this woman's eyes. I could tell that it was all she could do to keep from falling apart. She squeezed my hand before continuing.

"I want to tell you that when Jennifer died, I wasn't ready to forgive you. I wasn't ready to let go of her. And I felt that if I gave you forgiveness for what you did, then I would betray my daughter."

She paused to take a deep breath. Her husband rested his hand on her shoulder. "We just came here to let you know that even though everything is different now, we forgive you." She looked me in the eyes and said those words.

My jaw dropped. Then the tears came. I was in absolute shock. Memories of the accident sped through my mind. I recognized all the pain I had caused a long time ago, yet I still can't understand what this woman just said. "You forgive me?" I whispered, so quietly that I was afraid they couldn't even hear me.

Jennifer's mom smiled. She pulled me so close to her that I couldn't breathe. And then I cried. I cried so long that I didn't even hear the police officer come into the hall to tell us that they were ready to begin. We held each other for a few more seconds before letting go, then walked into the courtroom, together.

KAREN

"Thank you, Lord," I whispered as I took my seat beside John in the courtroom. I felt happy. For the first time since Jenny died, I felt happy. A weight had just been lifted from my chest. I watched as Carley took her seat next to her attorney. She was such a little girl—and to think I hated her. I was ashamed of myself. She turned around in her seat to face me and she smiled. I returned the glance, and she swiveled back to look at the front of the room. The back door of the courtroom opened, and the judge appeared.

"All rise," the officer recited. And we began…

About forty minutes into the trial, the events of the crash were rehashed, and the judge finally understood what the police found. Carley sat in her chair. She looked so weak and fragile, like at any moment she could break into a million pieces. All of a sudden, the judge called out to me. "Mrs. Crawley, I would like to encourage you to take the stand at this time."

I stood up uneasily. John grabbed my hand as I walked past him. "You can do this," he whispered. I shuffled to the front of the room, taking the stand next to the judge. I began to feel nauseated, so I offered up a silent prayer before turning to face him.

He smiled at me sympathetically and said, "I know this is a hard time for you, Mrs. Crawley, but it is necessary to get your feedback on what the outcome of the trial should be. I would like to ask you now, is there anything you want to add in order to possibly sway me on my decision of punishment for Carley Jameson?"

I took in a deep, raspy, breath.

"My daughter Jennifer was my pride and joy, as well as my husband's. She had such a peace about her, that whenever she entered a room, everyone would feel calm. She had that gift. Jenny hated arguing. She avoided conflict at any cost. Oh, and she was selfless. If she ever stopped to do something for herself, then I never knew about it."

I paused and looked toward John as he wiped a tear from his eye. "When Jennifer died, a piece of me went with her. I wasn't the same person, you can ask anyone. She was my light. She was my everything, and when she left, I was no more. Sometimes I would wonder if God was even there. I doubted so much in the past couple months. You could say I lost all my faith. But then my husband helped me to realize that God did not do this to us. He helped me understand that even though Jennifer is gone now, we will see her again one day. My husband showed me that there can be love, and hope, and life, after you lose someone. John let me know that just because Jennifer died, doesn't mean I have to. And I believe this has made me stronger. There is nothing I wouldn't give to have my daughter back with me. There is nothing in this world I wouldn't do."

I paused once more, taking in a deep, shuddering breath, and turned my head. Carley was staring up at me from her seat, eyes red and puffy, remorse penetrating through her. "But there is one thing I want to tell you right now. Carley Jameson made a mistake. She made a bad decision, but I know she is not a bad person. In fact, I think Carley is a very sweet and genuine young woman, and I am sorry that this happened to her."

I paused when I heard the judge gasp. He excused himself and encouraged me to go on. "Carley," I began again, now directing all of my attention to her.

"This is not your fault. And if anyone in this room decides otherwise, then I want you to know that John and I will always be here for you, because we all make mistakes. Some bigger than others, but mistakes nonetheless. I am sorry for what you went through, as I know you are for John and I, but there is nothing we can do to bring Jenny back. I pray that we will all be able to heal and move on, but I know it's going to take some time."

Turning back to the judge, I continued, "I want to ask you to go easy on Carley, because as I said before, she's not a bad person. My husband and I are trying to move on, and Jennifer wouldn't want Carley to lose everything. She wouldn't want that for anyone."

I paused, waiting for someone to say something. The judge shifted uncomfortably in his chair and was quiet for a few moments before thanking me and pointing back to my seat. When I reached the pew, John took my hand and kissed it. I looked at him and smiled, and I watched as a glistening tear rolled down his cheek.

It was times like these when I knew Jennifer would never be forgotten. She was here with us always.

CARLEY

I was sitting there crying beside Heather because I felt terrible. Mrs. Crawley just stood in front of a judge and told him how good of a person I was. *Wasn't her testimony supposed to be under oath?* I thought to myself. She asked him to go easy on me. I couldn't believe that. I took everything away from her, and she gave me everything I wanted. What kind of people were they?

They were the Crawley's. I know that much. Jennifer was just like her mom, sweet and kind, and she never stopped caring about me, even when I stopped caring about her. She was always there to help, and I knew no matter what, that if I ever needed her, she would be there for me.

So what kind of person does that make me? An awful one, that's for sure. I killed Jennifer Crawley, the one girl who was always there when I needed her, the one girl I was so jealous of. She was the one I needed to talk to the most right now. And she's gone, just like that. A split-second decision to get in that car drunk changed my entire life. It changed everyone's life, and no matter how much I want to take it back, I never will be able to forgive myself for what I've done.

Jennifer's parents forgave me. They wiped my slate clean. And not only did they forgive me, but they offered to help me if I ever needed it. These people were the kindest I had ever met, and I couldn't understand why.

So as the judge droned on in front of me, I tuned him out. And all I could hear was the music from that night. All I could see was Britney and I getting into my car and driving away. I saw Britney turn up the volume on the stereo, and I watched as she danced in the seat next to me. Then I started to cry because I know what was about to happen. I knew how this was going to end, and it scared me so much that I had to open my eyes. Because if I saw that crash one more time, if I heard the screams and twisting metal, if I saw any more blood, then I would've died. That overwhelming pain was consuming me like an inferno. I just couldn't breathe. I was trying to heal, trying to cope with everything, but the Crawley's forgiveness ruined everything.

How can they forgive me for this? How can they be so nice to me? I took Jennifer away from them. She's gone, she's dead, and she's never coming back. And they knew this, yet they had still chosen to forgive me. The problem was, I just couldn't forgive myself.

KAREN

I was sitting patiently in my seat next to John, waiting for the judge to reach his decision. I looked over at Carley. She was sitting in her chair, shivering. I knew she must have been worried, but hopefully my testimony swayed the judge's decision. When the judge cleared his throat, I was all ears. Carley lifted her head slowly, depressed, defeated, and afraid.

"After reviewing the case and listening to the testimony of the family of the deceased, I have reached my judgment. Carley Jameson, I honestly don't think jail time is going to do you any good. I think that you need hard work and guidelines. Therefore, I have decided to assign you to one thousand hours of community service for one year. If your hours are not performed in the allotted time, you will be going to jail when I see you again. You have one year, Carley. That's 365 days to straighten up.

"I'm also putting you on twelve months probation. If you violate any of the guidelines in the next year, you'll be put in jail. Carley, I hope I'm making the right decision. I hope you understand that what you've done is irreversible, but I trust Mrs. Crawley's judgment, and if she thinks you're a good person, then you must be.

"Make something of yourself, Carley. You have too many people who care about you." He pounded the gavel on the wooden table in front of him, signaling the end of the trial.

John rose up beside me and then waited. He was waiting for me to stand up too. This was where the suffering ended, and the healing would begin. Well, at least for us.

I looked over at Carley, as her mother weakly embraced her before standing up and making her way out of the courtroom. When I looked into Carley's eyes I saw something. Sadness. So much sadness. And I saw regret. In her eyes, I saw that Carley's suffering was just beginning.

CARLEY

I couldn't breathe. I felt like I was being crushed by something much bigger than myself. I felt like at any moment this weight that has been pushing down on me would force me to vanish in thin air. I knew this feeling. I have been feeling this way ever since the accident. Guilt. But this time, the guilt was at its worst. I was learning to deal with it. I was pushing it all the way to the back of my brain, but after my sentencing, this awful guilt has been pounding in my ears.

"We forgive you." Those words kept replaying over and over again in my mind. *They forgive me? Why?* That's the one thing I would never understand. I was taken by surprise when I saw Jason practically tripping up the aisle to hug me. He threw himself on top of me, wrapping me in a fierce hug. I stayed there for a moment, intertwined with the only thing keeping me here on earth.

"Thank God it's only community service," he whispered. I gently pulled back to look him in the eyes.

I paused for a minute before saying, "Jason, it will never be *only* community service. It will never be *only* anything. My whole entire life will always be centered on the fact that I'm still here and Jennifer's not." I stared intently into his eyes.

He quivered under my scrutiny. "I…I…didn't mean it like that," he said, unsure of himself. Or was he unsure of me? I had changed so much since that night.

"I know," I reassured him apologetically. "I'm sorry. You've been nothing but supportive, and I've been awful to you." I stared down at my feet.

Jason took my chin in his hand and lifted up my head to his eyes once again.

"Jennifer's gone, C. She's gone, and no matter how much you beat yourself up over it, she's never coming back. It was an accident; that's all it was. An accident."

I could feel anger rising up through me once again as I contemplated Jason's words. Then, after a moment of searching, I finally found the right thing to say. "What if it was me who died that night?"

Jason froze. I could see his face growing red, and I could see his ears start to burn as I watched anger rise in him as well. "If you died that night, I'd kill the person who did it." Just the answer I expected.

"Jason, that's the problem. That's why I can't deal with this. If they hated me, I would probably feel better! If they wanted to kill me, I wouldn't feel so guilty! But they don't, Jay! They don't hate me, and that's what makes them so much different than us. They have the power to be able to love someone who ruined their lives, and I can't handle that. I can't go through my life thinking that I am forgiven by these people, when I can't even forgive myself." I sat there, breathless.

Jason shifted from one foot to the other, staring intently at the ground. "I don't know what else to say, C, except that I will never be able to understand what you're going through. I've sure tried, but you just keep pushing me away. Carley, I don't want this to end, so I'm going to walk away right now. I'm going to take a break and let you sort through everything. And when you feel better, give me a call." He turned around to walk away, a bit of hesitation in his step. I could see in his body movement that he was waiting for me to call out his name. For me to tell him to come back so we could be together again. He was waiting for me to say I'm sorry and to tell him how much I loved him. But unfortunately, he was waiting for the call that would never come.

As I watched him walk back up the aisle, I felt something break inside of me. Like something shattered into a million pieces. It must have been my heart, because honestly, I'd never felt more broken in my entire life.

KAREN

As I was walking down the concrete stairs of the courthouse and out to our car, I caught Carley out of the corner of my eye. She was walking alone, her attorney paid and long gone. Her mother was far ahead of her. I felt a stab of sadness in my heart as I watched her head hanging low and her feet dragging on the ground. Her mother looked the same, just faster. Neither of them spoke to one another.

I began to think how lucky Carley's mother is. I began to feel jealous of the fact that her daughter was here, and mine was not. And I started feeling so angry with her because of her careless attitude toward her daughter. I wanted to run up to her and shake her and tell her how fortunate she was to still have Carley with her. I wanted her to realize that she has everything I ever wanted.

I tapped John on the shoulder, and when he turned around, I said, "Hey, John, I'm going to meet you at the car in a minute. I have to take care of something first." He nodded knowingly and said, "Okay. I'll be waiting."

He kissed me lightly on the cheek and smiled as he walked toward our car. A spark shot through me as I realized that John had love in him again. I laughed to myself, and I looked up to the clouds above me. "Thank you, God. You have shown John and I what true love is. You've held us together through all of this, and you've made us so much stronger."

After my quick prayer, I spotted Carley once again. Her mother had already reached the car, yet Carley was still trudging behind. I walked quickly to Carley and called out her name. She turned her head, pure grief engulfing her. I could see it in her eyes. She looked like everything she once was has left her. She looked like a shell—a shell of emptiness, nothingness. She was hollow. I don't know why this mood surprised me. I expected a happier reaction from her once John and I offered our forgiveness. Yet there she was, alone in this world, with no one to help her get through it.

Then, the most miraculous thing happened. Carley walked toward me and stopped nearly inches from my face. Her eyes were watered with tears, and I saw something hidden in them. A small spark was hidden somewhere in this girl, something inside of her that was dying to feel alive again. I couldn't help but get this feeling in my gut that told me I was the only person who could help her find it. I felt an attachment to Carley. Something that drew me to her, made me feel like I had a purpose again. Maybe God was showing me that it was my turn to do something. Maybe my purpose was to play a bigger part in Carley's life than she played in mine.

Carley reached toward me and embraced me. "I'm sorry. I'm just so sorry." She was weeping into my new satin blouse, but I didn't care. I felt so much compassion for this lost little girl. She cried desperately in my arms, and all I could do was hold her. All that was left to do was just listen. She had been ignored too many times. She had been hurt and turned away, and I could almost hear God whispering in my ears, "Love her. Let her know someone still cares for her. Let her know that I will always care for her." I don't know where those words came from, but I heard them over and over again in my head.

"Carley…" I began to speak as I gently pull her away from me. "I have forgiven you. I will not hold any harbored feelings toward you, nor will John. We forgive you, sweetie. Now you just need to forgive yourself."

She sniffed and then wiped her running nose with her shirt sleeve. Her eyes were red and puffy, and it wasn't long before I heard footsteps coming in our direction. I glanced up to see Carley's mom.

"Listen, Mrs. Crawley," she began, with a hint of irritation in her voice. "I am terribly sorry for your loss. I regret ever letting Carley get that out of hand, but we don't need you constantly on our backs telling us how you've forgiven Carley. Because obviously you've just made things worse. I would appreciate it if you would stop all of your preaching, because Carley and I will be just fine. We *are* just fine. So please, leave us alone, and we will do the same for your family."

Mrs. Jameson motioned toward Carley that it was time to go. I watched in awe as the robot daughter followed her mother toward the car. But before she could get too far away, I pulled out my business card and slipped it into Carley's hand. "Call anytime," I whispered. She nodded politely and walked away. And with her, I felt a piece of my heart float away as well.

There was a reason that Jennifer left this earth so young, and I was determined to figure out what that reason was.

CARLEY

The car ride home was quiet. My mom sat in her seat, steering the wheel robotically. That's all she's become— robotic. She doesn't laugh. She never smiles. She's empty. And I blamed myself. We were both empty. I could feel it inside me, this nothingness. I longed to feel whole again, loved, and cherished. I turned the business card that Mrs. Crawley handed me over and over again in my hands. I tried hard to keep it out of the sight of my mother. *What if she can help me?* I asked myself. *What if Mrs. Crawley can make me feel alive again? She seems to be the only one who still cares about me.*

But then I stopped, because I soon realized that no one ever truly cares. No one ever gets over something that ruined their lives, and no one ever truly forgives the type of people who kill their only daughters. So that's why I couldn't call her. I just couldn't face the woman who knew so much about me and still wanted to know more. I guess I just couldn't be around someone who constantly made me feel like something is missing.

Every time I was around Mrs. Crawley, or Jennifer for that matter, a gaping hole would appear right in my heart. I would always feel like something important just wasn't there. Yet those were the only times when I noticed it, whenever I saw the Crawley's. They seemed like such a perfect family, until now. Now, there were just two of them. And it was all because of me.

When we pulled up in the driveway, my mom turned off the car and, surprisingly, stayed still in her seat. I turned to look at her and was shocked to see tears pouring from her eyes. She looked at her knees and fiddled with her fingers. I sat in silence, afraid to speak.

"I don't know what I have ever done to deserve this," she whispered. "I'm not such a bad person, am I?"

I sat there, stunned. My mother was falling apart in front of me. Tears poured in monsoons down her face. I hadn't seen my mother this way since my dad left. It broke my heart.

She stared at me with hard, cold eyes. "I'm sorry," she whispered, almost too quiet. "Please get out of the car." Her head turned back away from me and stared blankly out the front windshield.

"Mom—" I began.

"Just go. Please. I have to go somewhere right now. I can't be here." She wiped away at her tear-stained face, smearing eye makeup all over her shirtsleeve. I sat there for a few minutes staring at this strange woman next to me.

I remembered some of the times we shared when I was younger. I remembered my mom on my seventh birthday. She bought these amazing princess costumes for me and all of my friends. Then she dressed up in a servant costume and waited on us hand and foot. It was such a fun birthday, and it's one I will remember for the rest of my life. Times like those seem to fade in the background as I get older. I never thought special moments like that could ever be forgotten, but in my heart, I know it's only a matter of time before those memories are gone forever.

My mother's heart was breaking. I was being ripped to shreds by my very own guilt, and love had no place in my heart anymore. I was alone. I was ignored. I was forgotten.

KAREN

I was sitting at the Sunday morning church service with John next to me as we listened to the pastor's sermon for the day. His words floated around the room beautifully, resonating with ever softly-spoken syllable. I heard the truth in them.

He began to talk about God's plan for us all. When he mentioned the topic for the day, I leaned a little bit closer, careful to hear every word he was preparing to say. "In all my years of mentoring, I have never once fully understood the reason for some of the problems my friends face. They come to me with terrible issues that can only be described as unforgivable. Sometimes, they are the ones doing certain things, and other times, these awful things have been done to them. I used to ponder why God would allow these horrendous occurrences to affect the ones he proclaims he loves so dearly. I honestly don't think I will ever be able to fully understand it.

"There is one person who comes to mind when I think of the word *unforgivable*. Her name was Cassandra. She was twenty-three years old when I first became her mentor. We met on one of the missions trips to the women's prison last fall. Cassandra was a troublemaker, I guess you could say. She was sentenced to life in prison because of a murder she committed not too many years before. She killed her ex-husband. She told me that it was because she was afraid of him. Cassandra lived in terror for two years, dreading the days he would come home from work. She said she tried to divorce him, and no matter how much she wanted him out of her life, she couldn't bring herself to file for a restraining order. They had two children together, and she was determined to make it work for them.

"So Cassandra dealt with the emotional pain for another year, until finally, she couldn't take it. All it took was the simple hiring of a hit man to do the job. Cassandra expressed her feelings of disgust toward her ex-husband, her feeling of hatred for herself, and the strongest feeling of guilt for making her very own children parentless.

"She cried to me many times during that first meeting. In fact, I think I might've shed a few tears as well. But while she told me her story, I prayed silently. I asked God to give me exactly what this woman needed. I asked him to speak to her through me. And he sure did."

The pastor chuckled. "Soon, I was holding this young woman in my arms praying over her. We sat there for hours, eyes closed, heads bowed, talking to the one person who could make everything better for her. Cassandra chose to allow Christ into her life that day."

He paused as a chorus of amens erupted from the congregation. "You know, there's something so amazing to me about how God works in people's lives. Even though we don't always understand why things happen, we know that God has a reason for everything. We know that we were not stuck on this earth for nothing. We are here for a purpose. All of us."

John glanced at me out of the corner of my eye. We were both thinking the same thing.

The pastor flipped a page of his notes on the podium and began again. "The most important thing I learned when dealing with Cassandra is how guilt can consume us in so many ways. It can overpower us, and it will continue to stifle our hopes, dreams, and goals until we learn to deal with it. Cassandra felt guilt because of what she did to her ex-husband. She felt guilt because of what she did to herself and her family. Cassandra was a guilty woman until she accepted Christ. The day that I met Cassandra, she walked in as a bitter, regretful, and broken girl. Cassandra left that day a refined, strong, and faithful servant of the Lord." He bowed his head, almost as if in remembrance.

"I must tell you all now that Cassandra's guilt was different from most of ours. You see, Cassandra's children and family are all followers of the Lord. And after the murder, her family told her that they forgave her for what she did. Her family *forgave* Cassandra for something most might think of as unforgivable.

"Well, in the Good Book, the Lord expresses forgiveness as a powerful tool. He knows that it's not easy to forgive, but we must. And Cassandra's family did just that. But still, she held guilt in her heart. And from that experience, I learned that guilt is not something that can be washed away by the forgiveness of earthly people, but by God himself. God is the only one big enough to wash away all of our wrongdoings. He is the only one who can heal us. And he healed Cassandra.

"Today, Cassandra still maintains her faith in the Lord. She has joined the outreach ministry for the prison, and she speaks at different events to people, mostly high school students. It's amazing what God does for us. Just look up at that picture right there." The pastor points toward the big picture in the front of the stage that hangs there during every church service. It is a large picture of a cross, and on it lies the broken body of Jesus.

The picture broke my heart every time, but it always reminded me of God's merciful love. And I found so much strength in that. I squeezed John's hand as chill bumps raced up and down my spine.

The pastor looked at the congregation. "Let God be the one to call you to do great things. There is a reason and a purpose for everyone and everything. It's not our job to find it, but to fulfill it. May you all go in his peace today."

The congregation stood up slowly and began to strike up a small volume of chatter. John and I rose up steadily and headed for the door. But before we left, I took one more glance at the picture at the front of the room. And then I thought that it's time to fulfill my purpose.

CARLEY

The phone sat across from me, silent, dead, but so loud at the same time. It begged me to touch it, to reach out and pick it up. Everything inside of me was pushing me to make that call to Mrs. Crawley. But there was still one part of me left that wouldn't dare do such a thing. I haven't slept for days, since my mother left. She had been gone for three days. I didn't know where she was, or who she was with. All I knew was that she was completely gone. Mentally and physically, she could no longer handle herself.

Something had happened throughout all of this. Something that was irreversible. Something that, no matter how hard I try, will never be made right. I was afraid—afraid to call Mrs. Crawley, afraid to call my mom, afraid to talk to anyone. I didn't want to talk anymore. I even turned off my cell phone because I couldn't handle talking to any of my friends. I couldn't participate in conversations about the latest gossip at school or the new spring fashions. It all seemed so unimportant now.

Everything had changed since the accident. I've matured so much, but I lost my heart. I just wasn't happy, and I would have given almost anything to change that. Then I began to think to myself, *Would I give anything to be happy again? Would I really?* And my answer came quicker than expected. *Yes. I would.*

I stood up and walked away from the phone. The cabinet where my mom keeps all of our wine sat at my right. There was no lock. I opened up the cabinet and saw the rows of numbing medicine. If I drank enough, everything will go away. I could be happy again. I could feel alive, or at least go to sleep. That feeling of guilt was consuming me. I had to breathe, and that was the only way.

But as I reached for a bottle of red wine, I saw Jennifer's face. Calm. That's the only word to describe the look in her eyes. She was calm. I heard a faint whisper, and it wasn't long before I realized it was Jennifer speaking. She said, "Sleep, Carley. Go to sleep." My hand jerked back, and I slammed the cabinet door shut. My hands started to shake, and I suddenly felt tired.

The kitchen was dark except for the dim light above the table. Then, I heard Jennifer's voice again, repeating the same words. It was a soft whisper, and pretty soon I found myself on the couch curled up in a ball. I pulled the blanket lying on the floor over my shoulders, and I slept.

I couldn't remember when I finally dozed off, but the clock read 1:23 a.m. I wiped my blurry eyes and stood up. I was a little wobbly from lack of sleep, but I soon stumbled back into the kitchen. I poured myself a glass of milk and sat down at the table once again. The kitchen was still dark; it was too early for the sun to have risen just yet. The TV in the living room buzzed softly, providing me with a little bit of comfort. I sighed, and my head fell into my hands. I took a few deep breaths before reemerging from my slump.

The phone. It bored holes into my body, and I felt a sudden urge to pick it up. I reached out and touched the object in front of me. I held it in my hand, clicking in the numbers that match those on Mrs. Crawley's business card. I listened for the ringing to begin before hanging up. I repeated this action about three more times.

I felt like I wasn't even there. Like I was in some completely different world where I no longer had control of myself, but I was a member of the audience of my life. I was watching myself from a distance, penetrated by fear and despair. I was watching myself die. And when I finally began to realize this, I picked up the phone, and this time I didn't hang up.

KAREN

My cell phone on the bedside table rang one, two, three times before I hauled myself out of bed to look at the clock. One forty. It was too early in the morning, but the caller ID forced me to pick up the phone. I hit the send button and placed the phone to my ear. "Hello?" I whispered as I silently shut the bedroom door behind me. I walked down the stairs to the kitchen and sat at the table.

"Mrs. Crawley?" a soft whisper echoed in the phone. She was nervous. She was tired. I could tell by the quiver in her voice. It was Carley.

"Yes. Carley, is that you?" I asked. "Yeah, um I don't know why I called. I just need to talk to someone." Her voice was surprisingly monotone, yet very unstable, almost as if this were her last option. It scared me to think of what she would've done had I not answered.

I spoke soothingly into the phone, "I understand, Carley. Would you like me to come over so we can talk? I think it might be better if we speak in person."

"No, I'm sorry," she quickly answered. "I don't know why I even called."

But before she could hang up, I whispered something into the phone. "Carley, let me help you." I heard her heavy breathing on the other end of the phone. It was haggard. I could tell that she was already having problems, and I could only imagine what she was going through.

After a few moments of silence she reluctantly agreed. She repeated her address for me over the phone, and I quickly scribbled it down.

"I'll be there soon Carley," I said.

Carley replied, saying only one word before hanging up, "Okay."

I quickly grabbed my keys and purse and walked outside to my car. I drove for a few minutes up the road, and once I reached Carley's driveway, I offered up a quick word of prayer before opening the car door and stepping out into the wind-chilled night. The light on her front porch was on, but otherwise the house looked completely dark. Every window was black and showed no sign of life. I pulled my jacket tighter around me and walked up to her front door. She opened it before I even rang the doorbell. Her face was pasty white, and her eyes were sunken in like dark black craters. I felt a pang of guilt for not stopping by to check on her since the court date. I saw all that she had become in just three short days, and it worried me.

The blank, hopeless look in her eyes showed me a new side of her. She nodded at me and moved aside to welcome me in. I took the gesture and quickly stepped inside of her beautiful home. The kitchen was dark and empty, yet it was a mess. Papers were piled up everywhere, and dirty dishes were resting in the sink. She offered me a cup of coffee, but I declined. I sat down at their cherry wood kitchen table, Carley taking the seat directly across from me.

I waited for her to start the conversation. "Thanks for coming. I mean, I'm sorry you had to drive here this early in the morning." She glanced down at her feet underneath the table.

I hesitated before asking, "Where's your mother?" I watched a flicker of pain flash through her eyes. She was remembering something, I could tell.

She didn't look up when she spoke. "She left." Those two words seemed to use up every bit of strength this little girl had left. I saw every bit of juice draining from her almost empty veins. She sank down in her chair and turned a sickly green color.

"She left?" I asked. Carley nodded her head solemnly.

"When?" I questioned.

"About twenty minutes after my sentencing." Carley's eyes finally lifted up to mine when she said that. "She can't take it anymore. And how can I blame her? It's all my fault." I stared at this girl sitting in front of me. Her heart was breaking, and mine was breaking for her. Tears began to well up in her eyes, and it wasn't long before they began pouring down her face. She was releasing every emotion she had kept bundled inside of her in the past few months. I reached across the table and took her hand. She pulled away.

"Why are you forgiving me?" she asked. "How can you just forgive me for what I did? I *killed* Jennifer! Your daughter is dead because of me! And you're sitting here trying to make me feel better?"

Her words stung more than I had expected them to, but I refused to take them personally. She was hurting, and I understood her anger. I hesitated before speaking again. She shook with grief and disappointment.

"Carley, forgiving you was not easy. In fact, it was the hardest thing I've ever had to do in my entire life. But I had to do it. Don't you see? Jennifer would want it." I paused to check her reaction. Her facial expression was confused. I could tell she didn't understand what I had said.

Then, she spoke, "Why? Why wouldn't she want you to hate me?" Her lip quivered. I could tell that was all she wanted—to be hated. I knew that she felt that if she was hated by us, then the guilt would go away. I felt sorry for this girl in front of me, who believed that hate was the only form of healing for her.

I spoke softly, "Carley, Jennifer wouldn't want us to hate you, because God wouldn't want it either."

Carley lifted her head so her eyes stared intently into mine. "How can you believe in a God after something like this?" she asked, almost irritated, gritting her teeth. "How can you believe that he really loves any of us after what he did to us? How can you just forget all of that and still believe?" She seemed truly amazed at the fact that I still had an overwhelming amount of faith after everything I'd faced.

"Sometimes believing is the only way to heal. Sometimes you have to understand that you are no longer in control. Carley, God didn't do this to us. But he does have a plan for our lives, and losing Jennifer was a part of his plan. I can't tell you that good things always come from bad, because sometimes it doesn't always turn out that way. Although we must have faith that God will not leave us, and we must never leave him. He is the only one who is always there, Carley. The only one." Her eyes still bored into mine, but now with less intensity. I saw a moment of wonder in her, where I knew she was contemplating what I had said.

"I used to believe in God. That was before my parents got divorced. I used to go to church with them every Sunday. My dad was a real hard-core Christian, I guess you could say. He would always tell me how much God loved me, and he never stopped telling the story of what Jesus did for me. I used to believe that God was real, and that he was so great. Then, one day I came home from school to find the whole house empty. Everything was gone—TVs, furniture, clothes, everything. I was shocked. I ended up trying to call my mom, but the phone had been disconnected. My father left me and my mom alone, without a home and without any faith. He took that from us the day he left.

"It made me wonder if a man like my father, who claimed to love God so much, could do that to us, then what kind of person was God? Huh? Can you tell me that? Who is God to say that's okay? Who is God to do that to me and my mother?"

She paused, trying to regain her composure before speaking again, this time in a more hushed tone. "And the sad thing is, my dad wasn't the only one who left us that day. My mom's heart left; so did her soul. So after that, I just gave up. Why should I care about a God who could do something like that to me? I shouldn't. If God doesn't care, then neither do I." She scraped her chair across the kitchen floor and stood up in a fit of rage.

"I think it might be time for you to go, Mrs. Crawley. I'm sorry I wasted your time."

I stood up to follow her to the door, my heart calling to God frantically for the right words to say to this girl. When we reached the front door, I whispered, "Carley,

I won't ever understand why Jennifer had to die. I won't ever understand why your father did that to you and your mom. But one thing I know is that God doesn't want us to understand. He just wants us believe. He wants us to have faith in him and what he can do for us."

I turned to leave but before I did, I turned around and said, "And Carley, God is not like your dad. He won't leave you. It might feel like he already has, but he's been here the whole time. I promise you that."

Carley stood there in the light of the hallway and watched as I walked down the front steps out to my car. I heard the door shut softly behind me once I had reached the driveway. I stepped into my car and drove away, leaving a broken girl in my wake. All I could do now was let God take over.

CARLEY

I hadn't been that angry in my entire life. Who was Mrs. Crawley to preach to me about God? She didn't know what God had done to me! She didn't know anything about me! I stormed into the kitchen and opened up the wine cabinet. This time I wasn't stopping myself, and this time, I knew I wouldn't listen to Jennifer. I plucked the cork out of the bottle of red wine and filled up my glass. I didn't even hesitate before drinking the whole thing in less than thirty seconds. I continued to fill up my glass, and when I finally looked down, I realized the bottle was empty after only fifteen minutes.

Another bottle was quickly pulled from the cabinet, and in twenty minutes, it was completely gone. I stood up from the table and stumbled my way to my bedroom upstairs. Falling carelessly onto my bed caused me to get dizzy, sending my head into a wild whirlwind, but I didn't care. I felt like crying but the tears wouldn't come. I wanted to pray, but then I remembered what God did to me. I began to yell, "Why? Why did you do this? How can you say that you love me and then abandon me like this! God, please! Don't ever leave me again!"

Grabbing a pillow, I rammed my face into it as hard as I could, letting my salty tears bleed into the expensive silk fabric. I thought about what I had just said, and then

I remembered Mrs. Crawley's words. "God's been here the whole time."

I slowly lifted my head to face the doorway of my dark room. Through my blurred vision, I saw a figure reaching out to me. He was gleaming and clothed in white. His eyes were the prettiest blue that you could imagine, and his smile reminded me of glinting pearls. He reached his hand out to me and began to call out my name. "Carley," he said. "You're going to be fine."

I was confused by this. He inched closer to me, and took hold of my hand. And when he did, I felt an overwhelming sense of comfort. My heart fluttered, and I felt him picking me up. I rested in his arms as he carried me away from a world of darkness. In his arms I felt safe, and I whispered, "Forgive me, God."

He smiled so beautifully and looked deeply into my eyes. "My child, you are forgiven. You always have been." A rush of relief swept over me, and I felt no guilt. My heart wanted to fly away. I had never felt more alive. I smiled again at the man, and then he told me to sleep. I closed my eyes, and for the first time in years, I was filled with peace.

KAREN

"I've reached her mother, and she's on her way now. You saved her life, Karen." The doctor at the hospital reassured me by patting me on the shoulder. John sat next to me and squeezed my hand.

I smiled at the doctor and replied, "No, God did that."

The doctor returned a quick smile and walked away. John looked at me so lovingly and said, "You know, you amaze me sometimes."

I grinned from ear to ear when I heard this. "Thank you for believing me," I replied. I remembered back to earlier this morning after I left Carley's house. I had seen the wine cabinet door slightly ajar when I had gotten there. When I was about to leave, I was hesitant after hearing the anger in Carley's voice. Once I left, I got a bad feeling in the pit of my stomach. Something wasn't right, but I couldn't quite tell what it was.

When I got home, I tried to go back to sleep, but sleep would not come. After about thirty minutes of tossing and turning, I finally figured out why I couldn't sleep. I pictured the open wine cabinet and the irritation in Carley's voice. Something told me to go back to that house. I woke up John and explained what I knew.

We quickly jumped into the car and drove back to see if Carley was okay. We found the front door was unlocked, but before we went in, we rang the doorbell numerous times, to no avail. After about a minute, we opened the door and walked in. I checked downstairs, and John checked upstairs. It wasn't long before I heard John call out to me.

In a matter of seconds, he came down the stairs, carrying a limp Carley in his arms. I gasped at the sight of her. We rushed her out to the car and in about fifteen minutes, we were at the hospital.

So there we were, Carley in the back getting her stomach pumped of alcohol, John and I sitting there together, Carley's mother on her way, and God, in the midst of us all. We sat there for about five minutes more until we saw a tall, blonde woman enter through the sliding doors. She hurried toward us, a worried expression etched across her face. I stood up to meet her and explain to her what happened. Tears began to stream down her face, and she pushed past me to find a doctor.

When Carley's doctor emerged from her room, Mrs. Jameson met her head on. "Please! Let me see her!" she begged.

The doctor agreed and took her back into the hospital room to be with her daughter. "She's awake now," I heard the doctor mutter to Carley's mom, as if it mattered at all.

I stood up with John, and we walked to the window of the room. I watched as Carley's mom reached out to Carley and embraced her tightly. Carley and her mother sat together and cried. I could tell that they hadn't hugged each other in a long time. I watched as mother and daughter reconnected, and I thanked God with all of my heart. I nudged John, and we turned to leave them be. Carley was safe, and we had God to thank for that. We walked out the doors of the hospital happy, together. "I've never felt closer to God in my entire life than in these past few months," I whispered to John.

He squeezed me tightly and replied, "All part of God's plan."

I won't ever be able to forget my daughter, nor will I ever try. She was and still is my entire life. But through that experience, God had shown me that eternal love is forever. I had come to realize that good-bye didn't mean we won't ever see someone again. And most importantly, I had come to accept God's plan for my life. God had shown me that throughout anything I might face, I was never alone. He had shown me that forgive did not mean forget, but it meant to heal, and accept love once again. And through this, I had found myself, I had found love, and I had found forgiveness.

CARLEY

When I saw her hurry into the hospital room, I caught a strange look on her face. Fear, pain, and guilt. I watched the stranger rush to my bedside. She collapsed on top of me, pulling me into a tight embrace. "I'm so sorry, Carley. I'm so sorry," she cried.

Tears filled my eyes as I held her there. Soon, they began to flow freely down my face. I had never heard her apologize for anything, and that was all I needed to hear. I stroked her head softly and said, "I forgive you."

She cried so loudly that the nurses in the room turned their heads to prevent any awkwardness. But the stranger didn't care. It hit me then at that moment, I was not hugging a stranger anymore because every part of this woman hugging me, reminded me of my mother. My *mother*. I smiled to myself and hugged her even tighter. "I love you, Mom," I whispered into her ear. She stopped crying long enough to lift her eyes to meet mine.

"Sweetheart, I have never stopped loving you." She hugged me again and rested her head on my forehead. We sat there for what seemed like hours, holding on to one another, catching up on the love we had missed for all of those years. Then, my mom sat up and brushed her hair out of her tear-stained face. She smiled a broad, lovely smile and said, "Let's go home." I quickly nodded my head in agreement.

Three hours later, the doctors agreed to discharge me, and Mom and I were headed home, but not before stopping by the Crawleys' house. We had so much to thank them for. On our drive over there, I reflected on the image of the man clothed in white.

I didn't remember how I got to the hospital, but my mom quickly filled me in. When she said that Mr. Crawley found me upstairs in my room and carried me quickly out to the car, I began to think I imagined the man in white.

I turned to my mom. "He seemed so real, like he was right there. And when I talked to him, it's like he understood. He spoke back to me, Mom. He forgave me."

She stared at me, astonished, and then replied, "Sweetheart, Mr. Crawley said he couldn't even get you to open your eyes. You didn't say one word to him."

Goose bumps shot across my arms as I thought about what she just said. "Well, then how did I hear him talk back to me?"

"Carley," she began. "I can't believe I'm saying this, but I saw the same thing this morning when I was sleeping. That same man came to me and told me to go home and be with you. He told me that you needed me. I can't help but think that God saved you."

I was astounded to hear my mother say this, because she had been the first of us to give up on God after my father left. "Carley, I know that I haven't been the best mom, but through all of this, I think God has really spoken to me. I need to change. We both do. Will you at least try to work through things with me?"

I smiled and nodded my head, still shocked that my mom and I both had the same encounter. I leaned my head back on the headrest, and said, "Well I'm going to try and get some sleep before we get there." But I was really praying. For the first time since my father left us, I prayed. I prayed to a God that I had finally come to know again. I prayed to a God I thought I'd lost. I prayed to a God who had never left me in the first place. I told him how sorry I was for everything. I told him how thankful I was for his forgiveness, and I told him that I loved him. I asked God to help me grow stronger and build a deeper relationship with him.

After praying, I had never felt more relieved. But still, something inside of me wasn't quite right. I finally realized what it was. I got my mom's cell phone from her purse and typed in Jason's number. I decided to send him a quick text. I wrote, "Can't call you now. On my way 2 the Crawleys'. I miss u, and I'm sorry. Forgive me, Jay?" I hit the send button and put the phone back in my mom's purse.

When we pulled into the Crawleys' neighborhood, I looked for their house. Both cars were parked in the driveway. I followed my mom to their front door, pulling my jacket closer to my body. Mrs. Crawley answered the door, a look of pleasant surprise crossing her face. "Come in!" she exclaimed.

KAREN

I was surprised when I opened my door to see Carley and her mother standing together on my front steps. I quickly welcomed them inside. Curiosity consumed my brain. "Can I get either of you some coffee, tea, anything?" I asked.

"Do you have any hot chocolate?" Carley questioned.

I smiled and said, "I'll see what I can do." We began a small level of chatter as I made the coffee. John soon emerged from his office after hearing the conversation. The Jamesons smiled, and John took a seat at the table as well. Carley's mom was the first to begin the conversation. "Um, I just wanted to come by to thank you both tremendously. You have been such huge blessings in our lives, and Carley and I are so lucky to have friends like you. Both of you have honestly astounded me with how you've dealt with everything. After the accident, your quick forgiveness of Carley threw me off completely. I have just never been used to people who are so loving and genuine. You have both helped us so much more than you can guess. Carley and I are going to try to work through everything, because you've helped us realize that family is the most important thing."

She paused before continuing, "And I have to say one thing more. I am so terribly sorry for how I have treated you in the past few months. To be honest, I was jealous. The way you could still be happy after something tragic happened shocked me. When my husband left, I stopped being happy, and that is what ruined my relationship with you, Carley. And I'm sorry for that."

I reached forward and grabbed her hand. "You are more than welcome, and please don't apologize. Honestly, Carley has changed my life more than I ever expected her to. I am a new person, and so is John. Your daughter is something special, Mrs. Jameson, and she is something that should never be taken for granted. Never forget that."

Carley's mom nodded her head feverishly and then said, "This whole experience has taught me that much." She casted a loving glance toward her daughter, who smiled back at her. "I just want you both to know how sorry I am for the pain we've put you through, and I thank you tremendously for your forgiveness. God has worked in my life, and in Carley's, because of you what you've done for us."

I smiled back at her. "God revealed himself to you because he loves you both. He wants both of you to accept him and enjoy everything that he has to offer. I've expressed to Carley many times that God is the one person who will never leave us."

Carley's mom nodded her head once again, as a small tear worked its way to the brink of her eye.

I squeezed her hand a little bit tighter. "You are both welcome in our house forever. We know you as our sisters in the Lord now." I smiled.

"Thank you so much," Mrs. Jameson replied.

I turned my attention to Carley when I heard her clear her throat. I expected her to give a long, drawn-out speech of how she had changed, similar to her mother's.

Instead, she looked right at me and said, "Thank you for forgiving me."

I saw something new in her eyes, something that was never there before: hope. I could see such a bright future laying out right before her, and it made my heart burst with joy. I smiled at her, the young girl I had gotten the privilege of getting to know, and the one girl who God used me to save.

I couldn't save Jennifer. As much as it hurt me to realize, I knew it was true. But because of what happened to Jennifer, God was able to save Carley. Although it didn't bring Jenny back, it gave me more love, faith, and compassion than I could have ever asked for.

Carley and her mother stood up to leave, hugging John and I both before heading out to their car. Standing on our front steps, I watched them drive away, John holding me tightly in his arms. The wind blew softly, rustling the leaves in the front yard. I closed my eyes and said a silent prayer, thanking God for his eternal love and his infinite mercy.

When I opened my eyes, I saw my daughter standing directly in front of me. Her face was soft and more beautiful than ever. John saw her too. I was amazed when a man dressed in white appeared behind her. He rested his glorious hand on her shoulder and smiled with a smile of a thousand suns. His blue eyes were the color of the ocean, and they shone with immeasurable amounts of love.

Jennifer smiled at us and walked slowly away from the man in white, up to John and me on the porch. She stood before us, looking so real. I reached out to touch her face, expecting her to fade away immediately. Instead, she reached her hand up to hold mine to her cheek. She smiled, so beautifully. The man in white watched as mother, father, and daughter reunited.

"I am not far. I am not gone. I am always here," Jennifer whispered.

I gasped at the sweetness of her voice. She sounded like an angel.

"I love you both; I always will. I will see you again one day. Good-bye, Mom. Good-bye, Dad."

She slowly pulled away from my hand, but I was reluctant to let go. Soon, she was back with the man in white, who looks like none other than the man on the cross in the picture at church. John and I both knew who he was. "Thank you, Lord," I whispered. The man smiled and embraced Jennifer as she came back to him.

She smiled at us one last time, and as soon as another gust of wind raced by, she was gone.

I turned to look at John, completely amazed. His eyes offered no explanation. I hugged him tightly, and we turned to walk back inside together. We had come to accept God's plan for us and embraced it. We were no longer far from Jennifer, never far enough to forget, but we realized then that time would heal our pain and forgiveness would let us love again. It always does.

ONE YEAR LATER

Dear Mr. and Mrs. Crawley,

I thought I would let you both know how I'm doing my first year in college. Well, for starters, I absolutely love it! God has opened so many doors for me, including head of the Habitat for Humanity club at my school. I have been working hard with my team to provide homes for people who have nothing. It is such an amazing feeling to be able to present people with a house. I feel like this is my calling!

My mom is doing really good. She is loving South Carolina! She wanted me to tell you that she'll be in touch soon because she wants you both to come visit and see the new house. This year has really been a good one for me, and I am so grateful for all you both have done for me.

I also have some very exciting news. Jason and I will be getting married next fall! He proposed just this week! I would like to ask you, Mr. Crawley, if you would please walk me down the aisle? I know it's a lot to ask, but you are like my father now. And Mrs. Crawley, I wanted to ask you to be the maid of honor. It would mean so much to me.

Aside from that wonderful news, I have been talking to God lately about everything, and I feel like he has called me to do something great. An idea has been given to me, and I wanted to ask your permission. God has planted this idea for the creation of a Teens Against Drinking organization in my head. I have talked to a lot of friends here at school who would be willing to help with the funds, and basically it would be a place where kids can hang out without feeling the pressure of drinking. I wanted to ask your permission, of course, to name it in Jennifer's honor.

Please write me back, let me know how you both are doing, and let me know what you think. Thank you both again for the love and kindness you have shown me. God knows I didn't deserve it. But you gave it anyway. I am eternally grateful to you both.

I wish you all the best, and I love you both so much. I know that Jennifer is looking down on us all, and she's happy with what she sees.

Much love and many blessings,
Carley Marie Jameson

STUDY

Questions

1. The main idea of this book is learning to forgive the "unforgivable." Think back to when something unforgivable was done to you. How did you feel? Do you still feel the same after reading this book? Why or why not?

2. If you were Karen, would you ever have been able to forgive Carley for what she did? Why or why not?

3. How do you feel when you hold a grudge against someone?

4. Think back to a time when you felt like God wasn't around. What did you do? How did you react? Are you proud of yourself for the way you handled the situation?

5. Do you regret any decisions that you have made in your life?